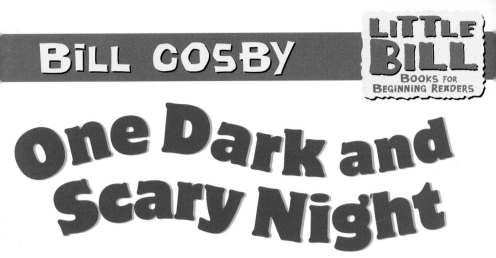

BILL COSBY

LITTLE BILL BOOKS FOR BEGINNING READERS

One Dark and Scary Night

by Bill Cosby

Illustrated by Varnette P. Honeywood

SCHOLASTIC INC.
New York Toronto London Auckland Sydney

Cartwheel B·O·O·K·S®

Assistants to art production: Rick Schwab, Nick Naclerio

Library of Congress Cataloging-in-Publication Data

Cosby, Bill, 1937-
    One dark and scary night / Bill Cosby; illustrated by Varnette P. Honeywood.
        p.   cm.— (Little Bill books for beginning readers)
    "Cartwheel books."
    Summary: One night Little Bill is convinced there are mean things in his dark closet and that they are just dying to get him. Only when Alice the Great performs a magical tucking-in trick do the mean things go away for good.
    ISBN 0-590-51475-X (hardcover)   0-590-51476-8 (paperback)
    [1. Fear of the dark—Fiction. 2. Great-grandmothers—Fiction. 3. Afro-Americans—Fiction.] I. Honeywood, Varnette P., ill. II. Title. III. Series: Cosby, Bill, 1937- Little Bill books for beginning readers.
PZ7.C81850n 1999
[E] — dc21   98-8813
                                                                                                   CIP
                                                                                                    AC
10 9 8 7 6 5 4 3 2 1   9/9 0/0 01 02 03 04

Printed in the U.S.A.   23
First printing, January 1999

To Ennis,
"Hello, friend,"
B.C.

To the Cosby Family,
Ennis's perseverance against the odds
is an inspiration to us all,
V.P.H.

Dear Parent:

A child's imagination, usually a source of delight, can also be a source of torment. Little Bill's trouble materializes one night when he's in bed. In his dark room, ordinary night sounds and shadows suddenly seem menacing. He grows convinced that something's lurking in his closet, waiting to get him. And he runs, screaming, into his parents' room.

His mother brings him back to his own bed and assures him that there's nothing in his closet. Little Bill knows she's right. But fact is no match for imagination, and he runs again, this time to his great-grandmother. She too returns him to his own bed. But she knows that a child can require something more powerful than logic to fight off an imaginary fear, especially at night. So before she leaves him alone in his room, Alice the Great shows Little Bill a magical way of fixing his covers to keep himself safe.

When a terrified child runs into your room at night, after you listen to his fears and comfort him, you can lead him back to his room and sit with him until he falls asleep, or you can let him fall asleep in your bed and then carry him back to his room. (If he's too scared to stay in his room, you can let him spend just this one night with you.) In the morning, you can sort out his fears—perhaps a disturbing TV show or anxiety about something in his life—and prepare him to sleep in his own bed the next night. A security blanket, "magic" object, or simple bedtime ritual often helps. And many children, on scary nights, will feel much safer if they're allowed to fall asleep with the light on, or can turn on a night-light in their room.

Alvin F. Poussaint, M.D.
Clinical Professor of Psychiatry,
Harvard Medical School and
Judge Baker Children's Center,
Boston, MA

Chapter One

Hello, friend. I'm Little Bill. Do you want to know about a scary story? It's a true scary story. It happened late one night...one dark and scary night.

My parents, my brother Bobby, and my great-grandmother Alice the Great were sleeping. I was alone in my room.

All alone.

My room was dark and quiet.

I saw a light moving along my
wall. What was this light? Who put
it on my wall? Maybe the light was
from the headlights of a car driving
by. Maybe not. Maybe it was
something else.

Then I heard a strange sound—thump, thump, thump—in my ceiling. Who was putting the sound in my ceiling? Maybe the sound was from a tree branch knocking against the roof. Maybe not. Maybe it was something else.

Again! The strange light moved across my wall.

The closet door was open. Open! Oh, no! I thought I saw something move in my closet. I thought I heard something move in my closet.

There's a thing in my closet!

I lay very still. I tightened every muscle in my body so I wouldn't move. I held my breath so the thing in my closet wouldn't know I was there. But my nose started to itch, my leg started to twitch, and my lungs were about to burst.

I jumped from my bed and, screaming, I ran down the hall and into my parents' bedroom. I crawled between them.

"I'm sleeping here tonight," I said.

"No, you're not," said Dad.

"Dad! You don't understand!" I said. "I have to sleep here tonight!"

"Did you have a nightmare?" my mother asked.

"No," I said. "Mom, this isn't a dream. This is real. Mean things are in my closet and they're going to touch me."

I had to talk fast because if you talk slowly, they send you back to bed.

Dad turned on the light. "The only mean thing in this house is me when I don't get my sleep," he said.

Chapter Two

Mom walked with me back to my room. She turned on the light and opened the closet door.

"No one is here," she said.

"That's because they saw you coming," I explained.

"Look, Little Bill. No things are in the closet. It's way past your bedtime and you have to go to sleep. You need your rest."

She helped me into my bed. I tried to make my face look scared, but Mom kissed me and turned out the light. But I didn't fall asleep because…the strange light crawled across my wall again and I thought I saw the thing move in my closet. I thought I heard the thing move in my closet.

I lay very still. I tried not to move—not even to breathe—so the thing in my closet—the mean thing with things to touch me and hairs coming out of its nose and ears (and it was wet, too)—I tried not to move so it wouldn't know I was there.

But my nose started to itch again, my legs started to twitch again, and my lungs burst! So I jumped from my bed and, screaming, I ran down the hall and into my great-grandmother's room.

"May I sleep here with you?" I asked. "A thing with things is in my closet—in my room—and I can't sleep there and I'm very, very sleepy."

I made my eyes all wide and fluttered my eyelids and made myself look helpless and needy and waited for her response.

"You're a big boy now," said Alice the Great. "You can sleep in your own bed. Come along." She grabbed her cane and we walked down the hall and back to my room.

She opened the closet door and poked around with her cane.

"They only come out when the lights are out," I explained.

"All right," she said. "Let's turn out the lights and we'll wait for them."

We sat in the dark on the closet floor among toys and games and sneakers. Pants and shirts tickled our shoulders.

"It stinks in here," I said.

"That's right, Little Bill," said Alice the Great. "No thing wants to sit all cramped up in a messy closet that's musty smelling—like mothballs and old sneakers."

We sat there for a while, but the thing didn't come.

Alice the Great pushed the door open with her cane. "Help me up, Little Bill," she said.

And I did.

"Now get back into your bed and get some rest."

And I tried, I really did. But my nose started to itch, and my legs started to twitch....

So I jumped from my bed and, screaming, I ran down the hall and back into my great-grandmother's room.

"The thing didn't come into the closet when we left because it was afraid of you," I said. "It can only come out after you leave."

"I see," said Alice the Great. "Then why don't you sleep in my room."

"Yes! I'll sleep in your room."

"And I'll sleep in your room!" she said.

No! "That won't work," I said. "They'll know where I am and they'll come into your closet."

Once again, Alice the Great led
me back to my room. She sat on my
bed and I sat, too.

"Why are they in your closet?" she asked.

"I don't know."

"Have they ever touched you?" she asked.

"No."

"Why not?"

"Because I run," I explained.

"Well, then," she said. "They're not so dangerous after all."

"I've just been lucky so far," I said.

"They don't get your mom and dad," she said.

"That's because they're a team. They protect each other," I explained.

"They don't get your brother," she said.

"That's because my brother is mean," I said. "They only want nice little boys like me."

Alice the Great put her arms
around me and gave me a big hug.
"You are a nice boy," she said.

Chapter Three

"Now, Little Bill," said Alice the Great, "I want you to stop thinking about bad things in your closet and start thinking about good things. Think about your friends. Think about tomorrow—playing and having fun. And, think about how wonderful tomorrow will be."

I wanted to do what my great-grandmother said, but I couldn't. I was sleepy, but I had to stay awake to be ready for the things.

And then she said, "I'm going to fix your blanket in a magical way so that thing never comes near you." She pulled my blanket off my bed.

"This is what I do with my covers," Alice the Great said, "so the things in the closet don't get me!"

Then she put the covers over me.

She pulled them up to my chin. And with the palms of her hands, she smoothed out the wrinkles.

And she said, "Good night, sweet Little Bill. May this magic keep the things from coming out of the closet. Get away, things!"

"Would you like me to leave a little light on?" she asked.

"Okay," I said.

"Would you like me to stay here until you fall asleep?" she asked.

"No," I said. "I'm all right now."

She kissed me and left the room.

I heard a car go by and I saw a light move across my wall. I knew that the light was from the car's headlights.

I heard a thump in the ceiling. I knew that a branch had fallen on our roof.

And I knew the thing couldn't hurt me.

Chapter Four

The next morning, nothing seemed scary with the bright sunshine coming in the windows.

"Did you sleep well?" she asked.

"I did," I said. "Now I know the magic. When I hear something, I'll pull up the covers and smooth out the wrinkles and think about my friends and having a good time."

"And the things will go away," she said.

"And the things will go away," I said. "Thank you for your magic, Great-grandma."

HOWARD L. BINGHAM

Bill Cosby is one of America's best-loved storytellers, known for his work as a comedian, actor, and producer. His books for adults include *Fatherhood*, *Time Flies*, *Love and Marriage*, and *Childhood*. Mr. Cosby holds a doctoral degree in education from the University of Massachusetts.

Varnette P. Honeywood, a graduate of Spelman College and the University of Southern California, is a Los Angeles-based fine artist. Her work is included in many collections throughout the United States and Africa and has appeared on adult trade book jackets and in other books in the Little Bill series.

Books in the LITTLE BILL series:

The Meanest Thing to Say
Can Little Bill be a winner...
and be nice, too?

The Treasure Hunt
Little Bill searches
for his best treasure.
What he finds is a great big surprise!

The Best Way to Play
How can Little Bill and his
friends have fun without the
new *Space Explorers* video game?

Super-Fine Valentine
The other boys are saying
that Little Bill is in love.
How can he stop them?

Shipwreck Saturday
Little Bill is proud of his
new boat. He made it himself.
But the older boys say it will sink!

Money Troubles
Little Bill needs $100.
How will he get it?